KILDEER BIRTHDAY
BOOK CLUB

Lainey Simanek
celebrated her birthday
on 3/2/2006
with the donation of
this book

One Sunday Morning
by YUMI HEO

Orchard Books / New York

To my son, Auden, who has brought wonderment and joy
to all my days

Copyright © 1999 by Yumi Heo
All rights reserved. No part of this book may be reproduced or transmitted in any
form or by any means, electronic or mechanical, including photocopying, recording,
or by any information storage or retrieval system, without
permission in writing from the Publisher.

Orchard Books, A Grolier Company
95 Madison Avenue, New York, NY 10016

Manufactured in the United States of America
Printed and bound by Phoenix Color Corp.
Book design by Rosanne Kakos-Main
The text of this book is set in 18 point Optima Medium.
The illustrations are collage and pencil and oil.
1 3 5 7 9 10 8 6 4 2

Library of Congress Cataloging-in-Publication Data
Heo, Yumi.
One Sunday morning / Yumi Heo.
p. cm.
Summary: Minho and his father have an active morning at the park, taking a carriage
ride, seeing the animals in the zoo, and riding the merry-go-round.
ISBN 0-531-30156-7 (trade : alk. paper).
ISBN 0-531-33156-3 (lib. : alk. paper)
[1. Parks—Fiction. 2. Dreams—Fiction.] I. Title.
PZ7.H4117Or 1999 [E]—dc21 98-41161

KILDEER SCHOOL
BOX 3100 RFD
LONG GROVE, IL 60047

One Sunday morning,

25Av 4 2
      3 N

Minho and his father took the subway to the park.

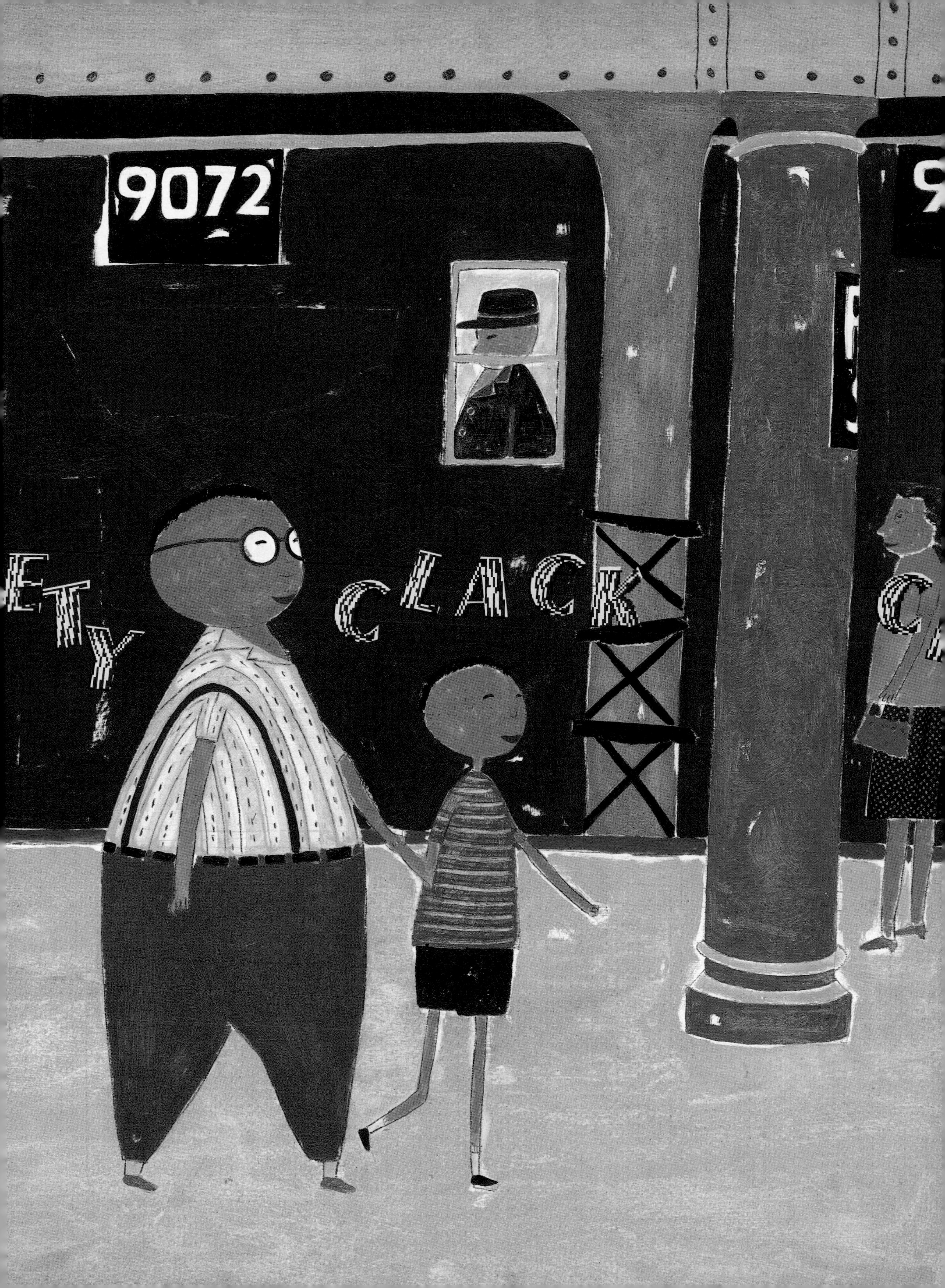
9072
ETY
CLACK

THUMPA

THUMPA

They walked along the paths. People were jogging,
riding bicycles, and roller-blading.

whirrrr

whirrrr

They watched people sail remote-control boats on the pond.

They went for a horse-and-carriage ride around the park.

RATTLE

RATTLE

CLO

CLIP— CLOP CLIP—

Minho's father bought a hot dog, a pretzel, and a soda for Minho.

They watched a man making balloon animals.

They walked to the zoo and watched sea lions barking for fish,

monkeys chasing one another from tree to tree,

penguins hopping in and out of the water,

polar bears floating in the big tank.

Inside a large room were tropical trees, plants, and birds.

Caw
Caw

Caw
Caw

After leaving the zoo, Minho got a cotton candy,
and they headed for the merry-go-round.

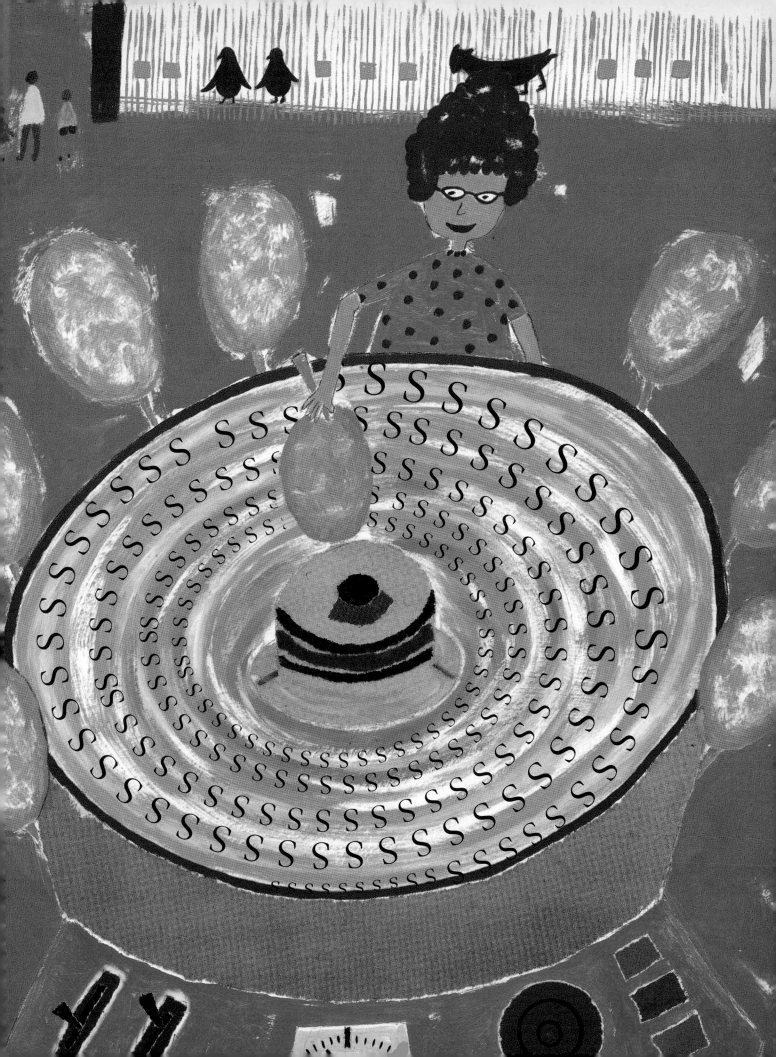

On the way, they passed a man playing a violin.

Oooooooaaaaa Ala-lah

Oooooooaaaaa Ala-lah

Minho got on the
yellow carousel horse,
and they went up and down and
around and around.

Minho began to laugh.

Ha Ha Haaaa

"Rise and shine!" said Minho's father as he pulled up the blind. "Oh no! It was only a Dreeeeeeeeeeam."